MEMOIRS OF SIN

Sis. Tiffany McNair-Jones,

May God continue to bless you.

Thanks for your support!

Memoirs Of Sin

by

Nikki Loyd

Copyright © 2005 by Nikki Loyd

Published by:
Voices Books & Publishing
P.O. Box 3007
Bridgeton, MO 63044
www.voicesbooks.homestead.com

Printed in the United States of America

All rights reserved. No part of this publication may be reproduced, stored in a retrieval system, or transmitted in any form or by any means, electronic, mechanical, recording or otherwise, without the prior written permission of the author.

Names, characters, places, and incidents either are the product of the author's imagination or are used fictitiously, and any resemblance to actual persons, living or dead, events, or locales is entirely coincidental.

Library of Congress Catalog Card No.: On File

ISBN: 0-9761410-6-X

ACKNOWLEDGEMENTS

Thank you to my Heavenly Father for putting this gift inside me and not letting me rest until I allowed Him to use me through writing.

Thank you to my husband Robert, who supplied me with the materials that I needed to make this book a success.

Thank you to my children whom, if I had not been at home taking care of them, this book may not have been written.

Thank you to my mother and dad who were the first ones to read *Memoirs of Sin*, all the way through.

Thank you to my family who were supportive of my efforts in this endeavor.

Thank you to Minister Stan for reminding me that I should be pursuing my God-given gift.

Preface

According to The Merriam-Webster Dictionary, the word "memoir" has several meanings. The first definition is cited in caps: MEMORANDUM. The second, also listed in caps is AUTOBIOGRAPY – usu. used in pl. For the third definition, "an account of something noteworthy: also, pl: the record of proceedings of a learned society," is cited.

For this book, the third definition is most appropriate. Here, the word memoir means an account of something noteworthy. It can be the record of proceedings of a learned society because sin cuts across all racial, socioeconomic and educational backgrounds.

The intention of this book is to minister to everyone who wants deliverance from the clenches of sin. If you want to be raised from the abyss of a lack of self-control; if you want to be released from impact of drugs and alcohol, if you want to be loosed from pornography, adultery and any other sin, this is the book for you.

There are seven memoirs (chapters) in this book. Each chapter depicts a sinner and their struggle. What follows is a discussion on how to get deliverance from that sin. All names, dates and times are fictional but the situations are real and represent anyone.

I pray that the readers of this book are encouraged in their Christian walk and to seek God even the more.

Introduction

What is sin? The Wycliffe Bible Dictionary clarifies sin: "Thus, a completely inclusive definition of sin would be: Sin is anything contrary to the character of God. Since God's glory is the revelation of His character, sin is a coming short of the glory or character of God (Romans 3:23)."

Some may wonder what sins are included in our coming short of the glory or character of God. Well, Ephesians 5:3-5 says, But fornication, and all uncleanness, or covetousness, let it not be once named among you, as becometh saints; neither filthiness, nor foolish talking, nor jesting which are not convenient: but rather giving of thanks. For this ye know, that no whoremonger, nor unclean person, nor covetous man, who is an idolater, hath an inheritance in the kingdom of Christ and of God."

Now what does all of this mean? Well let's start with the third verse. We see that fornication is listed. Fornication is simply sexual relations between two unmarried people. Notice that sexual relations include anything from orgasmic petting up to and including sexual intercourse. God intends for us to wait until marriage for all of it not just "the act."

Uncleanness is clarified in the Wycliffe Bible dictionary as, "profane, unclean, defiled, (from the Hebrew word tame'). So, uncleanness is something that is not sacred to our living God. It can be something that defiles, desecrates, perverts or contaminates (makes dirty) what is holy. For instance, having sexual intercourse while in the basement of the church, urinating on a Bible or spitting in food prepared for a pastor are all examples of uncleanness.

Covetousness is next. To be covetous is to desire what someone else has – something that does not belong to you; something that God did not give to you. Some people desire to look like someone else. Some people desire to have someone else's money, husband or wife. Some people desire someone else's position, fame or notoriety.

Filthiness is related to excrement (as mentioned in the Wycliffe). Excrement is a derivative of the word excretion. It means waste or can apply to fecal matter (feces). Needless to say, anything relating to waste and our consumption of it in any form is considered filthiness (When the prodigal son ate from the bottom of the pig pen is a good example of filthiness; Luke 15:16.).

An example of foolish talking is saying that you have put a bomb on a plane when you really haven't. Threatening to kill someone, ruin their credit or break up their home are all examples of foolish talking.

Jesting refers to harsh cruel "practical jokes" that hurt people's feelings. It's okay to laugh, have a sense of humor and joke with people. But here we are not to say and do things that scar a person's self-worth or self-esteem, all in the name of fun.

Verse five mentions that no "whoremonger" will inherit the kingdom of Christ. A whoremonger is someone who sleeps with ANYONE. They simply don't care about him/herself or the person that they sleep with. They have multiple sex partners whether at one time (like in an orgy) or a long list of sex partners (Some years back one particular basketball player was named as having had sex with over 2000 women!).

An idolater is someone who worships someone or (or holds something or someone more dear to their hearts) something other than Jesus Christ. Some people worship cars. They have to wash it all of the time rather than spending time with Christ. Some people worship pornography. They have hidden magazines and spend numerous hours on the Internet viewing pornographic images. Some people worship celebrities and go to concerts only to pass-out in shock at the very performance of their favorite singer.

Other sins are included in the book of Proverbs. They are the seven things that God hates. In Proverbs 6:16-19, the Word of God says, "These six things doth the Lord hate: yea, seven are an abomination unto him: A proud look, a lying tongue, and hands that shed innocent blood, An heart that deviseth wicked imaginations, feet that be swift in running to mischief, A false witness that speaketh lies, and he that soweth discord among brethren." These are the actions and attitudes that God rejects.

Let's more closely examine the things that God hates. First of all, God mentions that He hates, "a proud look." According to Proverbs, by J. Vernon McGee, this means, the literal "eyes of loftiness." This means that a person esteems himself to be more than he is. He thinks that he is superior to other people for whatever reason. He has a prideful attitude. He looks down at others like they are nothing and thinks he is superior. A proud look portrays the "big I and the little you," syndrome. It says that, "I am all of that and a bag of chips and you are just a half a bottle of Pepsi."

In the book <u>Proverbs</u>, J. Vernon McGee gave a brief commentary on the "proud look." He says, "It is the attitude that overvalues self and undervalues others. This is pride. It is that thought of the heart, that little look and that turn of the face, that flash of the eye which says you are better than someone else. God says, 'I hate it.' It is number one on His list – He puts it ahead of murder and ahead of drunkenness. God hates the proud look."

The second thing God hates is, "a lying tongue." In the book <u>Proverbs</u>, the author J. Vernon McGee, says it best when he describes what the Bible says about the "lying tongue." "Have you ever noticed that there is far more said throughout the Bible about the abuse of the tongue than is said about the abuse of alcohol? The abuse of the tongue is something that is common to all races and all languages. People talk about a tongues movement. There is a big tongues movement today. Do you know what that is? It is the lying tongue. How tragic it is!"

He goes on to say, "The psalmist (probably David) said, 'I said in my haste, All men are liars' (Ps. 116:11). Dr. W.I. Carroll used to tell us in class, 'David said in his haste that all men are liars. I've had a long time to think it over, and I still agree with David.' 'I'll admit that I agree with David too. Again the psalmist said, 'Deliver my soul O Lord, from lying lips, and form a deceitful tongue' (Ps. 120:2). In David's prayer of confession, he said, 'Behold, thou desirest truth in the inward parts: and in the hidden part thou shalt make me to know wisdom (Ps. 51:6). God is the God of truth. 'Into thine hand I commit my spirit: thou hast redeemed me, O Lord God of truth' (Ps. 31:5). How wonderful that is. How different from the lying tongue."

It is obvious that God wants us to tell the truth. One of the Ten Commandments clearly tells us not to lie. Everyone should take heed.

Number three on God's hate list is "hands that shed innocent blood." One of the most obvious examples that come to mind when considering the shed of innocent blood is abortion. Just think about any baby you know. How innocent they are. They depend on the mother with their very life. But a person with the wrong kind of heart can cause the death of a child.

What about the murderers? Some people are possessed by the devil and he fools them to kill people who have done nothing – people who have nothing to do with the anger and rage inside the murderer. In that sense they (the victims) are innocent.

What about people who murder with their tongue? They are just as hurtful because they murder the spirit. They say things to or against people that can kill their drive to succeed. They can murder the spirit in that they discourage people from striving in God. Those spoken words (verbal abuse or slander) can kill a person spiritually and many times that part of them can never be restored.

The fourth thing that God hates is, "an heart that deviseth wicked imaginations." What does this mean? I was listening to a minister one evening at church. He mentioned the seven things that God hates and gave examples of each. He talked about the issue of cloning and how it rests in the "heart that deviseth wicked imaginations."

Scientists who discovered cloning want to play God. They imagine what it is like to be God and to be a creator of a human being. Some of them have said out of their own mouths that as they clone other fruits, vegetables, or animals, they get to, "play God." They don't realize that they are biting off more than they can chew.

Another example of a wicked imagination is that of those who design bombs that will destroy the earth. Then those same weapons are stored and kept knowing that they cause mass destruction. The creators of these problematic tools don't care about the impact that these bombs will have on the planet – the planet where they too have to live.

God also hates, "feet that be swift in running to mischief." J. Vernon McGee said, "The heart blazes to the trail that the feet will follow."

I remember back when I was in junior high and high school. Whenever someone said that there was a fight we'd all quickly to run to see it. We would instigate, want to know who was fighting and who would win. We were, "swift in running to mischief." As youth we didn't realize that we were doing something that God hates.

God's Word says that He hates, "A false witness that speaketh lies." I was watching one of those court shows a long time ago. I think it was, "The People's Court" (the older version).

A mother had coaxed her daughter into saying that the father had molested her. The child got on the witness stand and said that he had fondled her. When it was the father's turn to testify he wept sorely. He held his head in his hand as he said, "I would never, never do such a thing. I would NOT do that." And he just kept crying.

They later went into the judge's chambers. The judge talked to the little girl. They came back out. She admitted that her father had not touched her and that her mother made her lie. The child said, "I'm sorry daddy. She *MADE* me."

The dad forgave his daughter. He didn't blame her. But he was hurt. This is truly why God hates, "a false witness that speaketh lies." It can cause so much pain.

The last item on God's hate list is, "He that soweth discord among brethren."

J. Vernon McGee said, "There are multitudes of folk sowing discord, and they are not all politically motivated. They are in your neighborhood, and chances are they are in your church. You may even have one in your home, and there is a possibility that he may be sitting where you sit. My friend, causing trouble between family members or brothers in Christ or fellow workers is something that God hates."

I know several people who are married and cheat on their spouse. In one example there was a couple that started having marital problems as many newlyweds do.

And all of the stress led to a separation. During their time apart one party slept with someone else. I don't remember how many times but it was at least once.

The couple is back together now and the other person doesn't know about the affair. A sower of discord would take this information and tell the unknowing spouse. This would cause uproar in the marriage (discord).

There are other things that displease God. I John 2:16 says, "For all that is in the world, the lust of the flesh, and the lust of the eyes, and the pride of life, is not of the Father, but is of the world."

What is lust? I see it as a strong, overwhelming, uncontrollable desire. So then, lust of the flesh is a strong overwhelming uncontrollable desire for someone's flesh or in laymen's terms: a desire to have sex with them. Lust of the eyes is a strong, overwhelming, uncontrollable desire to see something that you shouldn't like pornography. And the pride of life is going after the, "American Dream," no matter what the cost. In these cases, lust and the pride of life consume you and nothing else is important.

I am going to mention only a few more sins. There are many and of the ones that are listed we have all committed at least three (that's putting it mildly). I Corinthians 6:9-10 states, "Know ye not that the unrighteous shall not inherit the kingdom of God? Be not deceived: neither fornicators, nor idolaters, nor adulterers, nor effeminate nor abusers of themselves with mankind, nor thieves, nor covetous, nor drunkards, nor revilers, nor extortioners, shall inherit the kingdom of God."

The unrighteous are sinners. To inherit the kingdom of God means to die and go to heaven or receive His blessings while here on earth. Thus, we learn to die to ourselves, accept Christ as our Savior and Lord of our life. We do His will.

So, we've already discussed the meaning for the words fornicators, idolaters, adulterers, and covetousness. But there are a few more that we didn't address.

What does it mean to be effeminate? This simply means that a person is male and presents himself with female characteristics or mannerisms. He may flick his wrist a lot while talking. He may smack his lips between words. He may even go so far as to wearing makeup, a dress and carrying a purse.

Remember when I said that we all have committed at least three sins? Well, to those who have committed homosexual sins (men and women), you are not forgotten. With the issues of today concerning same-sex marriage, it is important to address those whom the Bible calls, "abusers of themselves with mankind." This refers to the sexual acts committed between those who are of the same sex.

A thief is someone who steals or takes what does not belong to him. It could be a material item as well as a person.

We've already talked about what it means to be covetous. So, let's move on to the drunkard. You may wonder, 'What exactly is a drunkard?'

A drunkard is someone who uncontrollably drinks and is addicted to alcoholic beverages. He or she consumes alcohol to the point that they are incoherent. He or she consumes alcohol on a regular basis. He or she is unaware of his or her surroundings. He or she is not able to control his or her actions. Simply put, a drunken person is not in his/her right mind.

Next, a reviler is a derivative of the word revile. Wycliffe defines it this way, "The English term appears in Mt. 27:39 where the Greek is blasphemeo, "to blaspheme" or "to speak reproachfully," "to rail at," or "to calumniate." This term is indicative of the contemptuousness of sheer irreverence for either God or sacred things."

So, a reviler has no respect for God the Father, His Son, His Word or His Church. He may say things referring to his hatred for the things of God. He may ridicule or call the things of God stupid or curse His name. He may even do vile things inside the house of God i.e. fornication.

Extortioners, according to The Merriam-Webster Dictionary, are those who obtain something by, "force or improper pressure," such as a bribe. So, an example of extortion is someone who bribes the pastor for a position in the church. An extortioner is someone who pays the dean at any given university to make sure that they receive straight A's on their transcript.

    Now that we have listed all of these sins (mind you there are more), lets figure out how to get away from them.

MEMOIR NUMBER ONE

Name: Dr. James Thurston, III

Age: 37

Occupation: College Professor

Sin: Lust of the eyes

Struggle: Pornography

     After a long day at Uphill University, Dr. Thurston returns to his office. He has a brief meeting with his graduate assistant. They discuss the assignment and determine when Dr. Thurston would like the term papers graded and returned to the students.

     After their brief meeting, the assistant and the professor leave. Dr. Thurston on his way out, stops to check his office mailbox. He had no mail. So, he prepares to leave. He walks out to the parking lot and gets into his $30,000 Mercedes Benz and drives home to his tri-level condo in the heart of the suburbs.

     It had started to rain. Dr. Thurston mentally prepares himself for a nice quiet evening at home with no interruptions.

     After about a 20 minute drive, Dr. Thurston pulls into his driveway and stops the car. The windshield wipers are swishing back and forth. It had begun to rain harder. It was thundering and lightening. He pressed the remote control for the garage door to open. Nothing happened. He thought that maybe he hadn't pressed hard enough. He pressed the button again. Still, nothing. That meant that he'd have to park on the driveway and fight the rain. 'Darnit,' he thought to himself, 'lightening must have hit and caused a power outage. Luckily I brought my umbrella.'

He pulled the keys out of the ignition, unlocked and opened the car door. He extended his left foot from inside the car, put his umbrella outside the car and opened it. He got out of the car, stood under the umbrella as he slammed the car door. While running to his front door he said, "Since it's raining so hard, I'll just use the keyless entry to lock the door from inside the house."

He ran to his front door, quickly unlocked it, went inside and shut the door. He wiped his feet on the floor mat then rushed to the linen closet to grab a towel to dry himself off.

'Hmmmm. I'm hungry,' he thought. 'What will I eat? Oh, yea, I'll eat that!'

For dinner he heats a frozen microwave dinner consisting of meatloaf, mashed potatoes and green beans. 'Mmmmm. This is pretty good.'

When he finished his meal, he threw away his trash and headed for his den/study area. He sits down in a huge custom made burgundy leather chair. He picks up the newspaper and begins to read it while smoking his pipe. After he finishes the paper he gets up to use the restroom. On his way back to the living room he hears the doorbell. He wonders who could be at the door, 'I'm not expecting any company,' he thinks to himself.

Nonetheless, he walks toward the door. He uses his left hand to hold the knob while he turns the lock with his right hand. He pulls the door open. Much to his surprise he is greeted by a very attractive female. "Hello," she says, "my name is Sally Miller and my car broke down at the corner of Elm and North Madison. I would use my cell phone to call someone for help but the battery is low and I can't make any calls. Do you mind if I use your phone?"

As she talks he, stares at her. His mind wanders. He never lets on as to what he's thinking about.

By this time it is pouring down rain. The young lady is sopping wet. He felt sorry for her and wanted to help her. He politely smiles, widens the door, invites her in and politely says, "Sure. Be my guest."

Sally smiles and says, "Thank you, Sir. You don't know how far I had to walk before I saw a house with a light on. I guess most of the power is out in this neighborhood due to the storm."

He smiles back and says, "You're welcome."

She didn't look a day over 19 years old. Thurston showed Sally to the phone. She didn't notice (or at least he hoped she didn't) how he was staring at her. Because of the storm, her clothes were sticking to her – revealing every curve that she might otherwise conceal.

"Yes. Single A Towing Company? My name is Sally Miller. I am stranded at the corner of Elm and North Madison. Can you send a tow-truck? Oh, good. I'll be waiting."

She hangs up the phone. "Well, that's it. They said they'd be here in about 30 minutes. But it will take me at least 30 minutes to walk back to the corner. So, I'd better get goin.' Thanks again, Mister. Bye…"

Before he could respond, she leaves and he closes his front door. 'She left so fast. I would have offered her a ride,' he thought, 'but I guess she'll be okay. I'll just watch her from the window – just to make sure she's okay – just until the tow-truck comes. Oh. Okay, they're here already. It's only been 10 minutes. Boy that was fast. Well, at least she's okay.'

He goes to sit down on the couch. He begins to think about Sally. She was absolutely beautiful. Her long wet curly blonde tresses hung just above her breasts. Her eyes were big, round and blue. Her lips were lusciously shiny.

The more he thought about her the more he thought about her voluptuous curves and he started to get excited. He wondered what she'd look like if she were undressed.

Immediately he goes to sit at his computer. He logs on. He begins with a harmless search about Single A Towing Company (this is his feeble attempt at trying to take his mind off of what he was previously thinking about).

Then it hit him like a bolt of lightening. He couldn't help himself. He surfs his way right onto a porn site. Before Dr. Thurston knew it, he had been sitting at the computer for three hours viewing forbidden sights of men and women in appalling positions.

After spending so much time viewing this material, he logs off. He goes to sit in his chair in his home office. He begins to get frustrated. He can't understand his own fascination with this deplorable sin. He doesn't want to be this way but he doesn't know what to do about it.

Then he starts to justify his sin. He says to himself, "Well at least I didn't touch her. And after all, I didn't design the website, I'm just looking at it. If they didn't want anyone to see it, they shouldn't have put it on the web. There are worse things that I could do."

Even after saying this, he still knew in his heart that it was wrong. His justifications were insufficient. He had struggled with the lure of pornography day in and day out for the last 17 years. His addiction interfered with many of his relationships. He was engaged three times to wonderful women but sabotaged each relationship for fear that they might find out his most inappropriate fetish.

It started when he was 13 years old. His older brother forced him to watch a porno flick. Ever since then he was never able to get those images out of his head. And, afterward the story of his life was all too familiar – the magazines – hidden under his mattress, in his socks drawer, his locker at school and other secret places. However, he never acted out until his first sexual experience at age 20.

He went to a nightclub and met someone whom he thought was a beautiful woman. He dated her for about three months. And then one night they committed "the act."

Looking back he should have seen the warning signs. He always had to wait for her to call him. He could never go to her home to pick her up for a date. Instead he had to meet her somewhere. After the date was over he had to drop her off at the same location.

One day she was at his house for a visit. They were snuggled up together on the couch. Suddenly, she had to go to the bathroom. And, that was the perfect opportunity for James Thurston, III to find out the truth.

Curiosity had gotten the better of him so he went into her purse. He was looking for anything that would give him more information about this beautiful yet mysterious woman. And lo and behold, he found a picture. It looked as if it had been taken at some nightclub. That alone was not so bad.

Thurston had to admit that it was certainly a very erotic photograph. The twists and turns depicted were all too familiar to Thurston. Thinking back to his initial viewing of a forbidden movie, it was like he could not get enough. He wanted more movies, more magazines, more phone sex and with the advancement of technology there was yes – the Internet.

But Dr. Thurston noticed something else about that picture. You see after years of viewing that kind of material, he had acquired a favorite "character," due to the types of acts she would perform. He was drawn to *her*.

Little did he know, the person in the picture was the same woman that he had watched in the porno movie a few years earlier. She was also the same mysterious woman that he had been dating for the last three months. And yes, she was the same woman in his restroom at that very moment.

All of this was such a shock. The woman that he was so drawn to before, was dreadfully repulsive to him now. When she came out of the restroom he told her that he felt sick. He told her that he would have to take her back to the undisclosed location where he had picked her up. After that, he cut all ties with her. He stopped calling, meeting and dating her. He moved to another state and he never told anyone of their relationship. He later found out that she was also a stripper and a prostitute at the nightclub where the photo had been taken.

Because of the relationship he'd had with (well, let's just call her Ms. Mysterious) her, he was usually emotionally distant in his latter relationships. And although, he cut off the relationship with Ms. Mysterious because he knew it was wrong – he realized something. He realized...that he took pleasure in it. He enjoyed the things that they had done – the sexual acts.

But he didn't want anyone else to know. There was a degree of shame that accompanied this type of thrill. He knew that others would find it highly disagreeable. If someone found out, he could lose everything he had worked so hard for. So, he put forth every effort to avoid being discovered. He found what he thought was a safe way to indulge himself – pornography over the Internet.

This brings us back to the present. We have a man wrestling with something that has become too much for him to handle. What must he do to relieve himself of this overwhelming burden? It was stronger than he was.

First of all, although Dr. James Thurston, III is very educated, he is not saved. That is what makes his efforts in the earlier description, "feeble." He was trying to combat this problem with his own human strength – to no avail.

So, the first step toward redemption is I John 1:9-10 which says, "If we confess our sins, he is faithful and just to forgive us our sins, and to cleanse us from all unrighteousness. If we say that we have not sinned, we make him a liar, and his word is not in us."

Dr. Thurston's deepest problem is unconfessed sin. He spent years trying to cover up his sin. He tried to hide from the guilt and shame that he felt. He didn't want anyone to know. Covering up, guilt and shame are all effects of unconfessed sin. And, as long as he did not confess his sin, he would continue in it. I John 1:9-10 shows that we are powerless against combating sin if we don't confess or admit it.

Dr. Thurston after admitting his sin would then need to accept Christ as his personal savior. Romans 10:9-10 says, "That if thou shalt confess with thy mouth the Lord Jesus, and shalt believe in thine heart that God hath raised him from the dead, thou shalt be saved. For with the heart man believeth unto righteousness; and with the mouth confession is made unto salvation."

And as Professor Thurston accepts Christ, he can then have a strong "tower of power," in Jesus to help him deal with the shame because Romans 10:11 tells us, "For the scripture saith, WHOSOEVER BELIEVETH ON HIM SHALL NOT BE ASHAMED." There will be no need for him to continue to feel ashamed.

Next, it is most beneficial to the Dr. to find a strong church. The Word of God tells us, "Not forsaking the assembling of ourselves together, as the manner of some is; but exhorting one another: and so much the more, as ye see the day approaching."

This simply means that we should go to church to find strength in one another – other believers. We are to exhort or encourage one another in the Lord. "As ye see the day approaching," refers to the day that the Lord comes and thus being prepared for His return.

As the doctor of philosophy gets his spiritual life in order, there are some practical solutions to his dilemma as well. First, it's wise for him to get some counseling from a **CHRISTIAN** psychologist. Much of his problem stems from his childhood and young adult years. He must confront those issues and begin to work through them.

Some advice from the counselor may include putting a block on the Internet at the professor's house. That way (at home) he is barred from all interaction with pornography via the web. Also, a support group for those with the same problem who foster accountability would be helpful. He would have to, "report" to them or kind of "check in" with the other people in the group. He would let them know when he was showing promise or improving. He would also have to let them know if he slipped back into his old habits. There would be consequences (determined and agreed upon by the group) if he violated his promise.

It is important for Dr. Thurston to remember that deliverance is a process. He may change overnight (after all, with Christ all things are possible). However, if he does not make an instantaneous miraculous transformation he must still stay encouraged. He must bear in mind that what took years to do may take years to undo. Therefore, it is a day-by-day process.

MEMOIR NUMBER TWO

Name: Antonio Rollos

Age: 27

Occupation: Male Prostitute

Struggle: Attraction to men

Sin: Abuser of himself with mankind

"How do I keep getting myself into these situations?" Antonio asks himself. Once again, he is in a car with yet another male "client" whom after receiving the sexual favor wants to kill Antonio for fear of being found out. He is in the car with a well-known pastor who's holding a gun to Antonio's head.

And once again, Antonio begs for his life. As he cries and screams, Antonio vows not to tell anyone. He pleads until the pastor is convinced. The driver takes "Rolly Tony" as he's called on the street, to an undisclosed, deserted location and kicks him out of the car.

This is not the first time Tony has had to walk for miles far away from home. He usually has to hitchhike/prostitute his way back home. Where's home? With his 89 year-old grandmother. She is bedridden and fades in and out of her right mind. She believes that her grandson is a security guard who works nights. She thinks that's the way he gets his money – because that's what he told her.

Tony has lived with his "Granny" ever since he was 12 years old. He was taken from his mother because she was physically, mentally, emotionally and sexually abusive. She used drugs and so did her many boyfriends who frequently sexually victimized Tony. Those are the things that made this strikingly handsome man homosexual. And, when he moved in with his grandmother, she was nothing more than loving and encouraging but it was too late for her love to make a big enough impact on Tony – he had already decided that he was homosexual and had not even a remote interest in girls. Granny did not know what to do about this and so she just pretended that it wasn't true.

Tony finished high school and began his first semester in college when one night after a big exam he decided to take a short cut home. He went through an alley. There were some drunken men who were "gay-bashing" before Tony had walked up.

They saw him. He saw them. He tried to run but they caught him. They grabbed him, undressed him from the waist down. You can imagine what they did next. It was horrible. They yelled horrible things like, "Since you want to be a woman, let me show you what it feels like to be a woman – faggot."

Tony just lied there in a puddle of blood. He cried for a while and then just stared off into space. He didn't know what to do. Someone came out and yelled, "Call an ambulance!" That was the last thing he remembered before he passed out.

When he woke up he was in a bedroom decorated in the "funkadelic" style – red beaded curtains, a zebra print area rug on top of an orange and yellow shag carpet, and a purple beanbag chair on the floor. There was a huge 6-foot-4, 250-pound caramel-colored man sitting at the foot of the bed dressed in drag. The man wore red lipstick, a blonde wig, a white negligee, and light pink satin high-heeled sandals.

He spoke with an intimidating tone. With a deep thundery voice, he told Tony that he had found him lying in the alley – incoherent. He brought him home and nursed him back to health and so there he lied.

This man went on to explain how Tony owed him for nursing him back to health and if he didn't pay monetarily, he'd pay with his life. This sparked fear in Tony. So, he made up his mind to comply with the man's wishes.

You see, this man who went by the name of "Keelo," was a pimp for male prostitutes. It was all a set up. The men in the alley worked for Keelo. They had been scouting for new "abusers of themselves." Without Tony's knowledge, they had been watching him for months.

And so that's how he ended up selling himself for money. That's how he ended up in cars with men who threaten his life if he tells anyone what they do together. That's how he ended up hitchhiking his way back home. And that's why he lied to his grandmother and told her that he's a night security guard. Tony knew that his grandmother couldn't bear to hear the truth.

So, now Tony is back home with Granny. As he sits down on the couch while she sleeps, he tries to sort through his problems. He takes a long hard look at his life. He tries to figure out what he's going to do – how he's going to get out of the prostitution game, get back into school and what it's going to take for him to turn his life around.

Tony doesn't realize that what it takes to turn his life around is Jesus Christ. But he will. Because while he was sitting on the couch with his eyes closed, taking a retrospective inventory of his own issues, the television was on. He didn't know that Granny was watching the Christian station while she waited up for him until she fell asleep shortly before he walked in the door.

On this night, the televangelist was preaching to all of those caught up in a life of prostitution. He had come to the end of his sermon and he was calling for the unsaved to come to the Lord. He said, "You may think that you have gone too far. You may think that you are in too deep. You might think that you've done too much. But tonight, I want you to know that you haven't. I want you to know that God loves you and He cares. I want you to know that Christ accepts you, as you are – broken, weary and torn. You want to turn your life around but you can't do it alone. Only Jesus Christ has the power to restore, renew, rejuvenate, replenish and rehabilitate. Only He is your strength. Won't you accept Him tonight as your personal Savior? Please say the prayer of repentance with me."

By this time Tony had opened his eyes. He heard this powerful message. And Tony proceeded to say the prayer of repentance.

Then the minister went on to say, "If you need additional prayer and/or counseling please call us at 1-800-PRAY-4-ME."

And Tony did. That was four years ago. Today Tony is a new **man** in every sense of the word. He is a true example of 2 Corinthians 5:17 which says, "Therefore if any man be in Christ, he is a new creature: old things are passed away; behold, all things are become new."

Today, Tony is saved, sanctified and Holy Spirit filled. He is a pastor at the local church where his ministry gears toward homosexuals, male prostitutes, victims of various forms of abuse, and teen runaways.

His road was long and hard. And he struggles daily but he is determined to not give up. He has gone through counseling so that he can stand when the enemy tries to tempt him with the wiles of his past. After his acceptance of Jesus in his heart Tony still wrestled with guilt. Through counseling however, he learned that if he stumbles at first he should repent and try again the next day. Then, when he succeeds he can reward himself.

Tony had to make efforts to control his thought life. Most sins begin in the mind. Therefore, he had to take up hobbies or do things that he enjoyed – things that had nothing to do with his former lifestyle.

Another step Tony took to improve his life was to start immediately. Tony took the minister up on his offer when he said for the television audience to call if they needed additional prayer and counseling. He didn't procrastinate. Prayer was and is key in his new way of life.

And there is another surprise. Tony has also been dating a nice young lady for the last 6 months and is planning marriage. God bless you to all of the Tony's out there!

MEMOIR NUMBER THREE

Name: Rhona Tillman

Age: 44

Occupation: High School English Teacher

Sin: Hands that shed innocent blood

Struggle: Her temper

    The former Mrs. Rhona Tillman (now divorced), upon your first meeting her, appears to be a kind, sweet, compassionate and patient woman – that's until you upset her.

    Her friends describe her as "The Female Incredible Hulk," and she doesn't seem to mind. She frequently says with an endearing smile, "Don't make me angry. You wouldn't like me when I'm angry."

    It's a shame however, that her horrible temper cost her a wonderful man who stuck by her for 15 years. He loved her dearly. He was there for her. He was able to tolerate her horrifying temper – until it had driven him to the "last straw."

    During most of her childhood, Rhona had a loving family. Her mom and dad loved each other and loved their children. But when Rhona's dad died when she was 15 years old, her life took a downward spiral.

    You see Rhona and her dad were really close. She talked to him about virtually everything. She was always going places with him. And, he constantly bragged on her because she was a straight 'A' student, a cheerleader and had been scouted by a couple of modeling agencies. He frequently told her, "Rhona, you're the apple of daddy's eye."

But Rhona's dad's death was a shock. To Rhona it happened all of a sudden. It seemed as if he was snatched away from her without notice – without her telling him how much she loved him – without her having a chance to say goodbye.

Rhona waited an entire year before mourning the loss of her father. And since the day her father died, the relationship between Rhona and her mother was nothing to get excited about. They argued constantly.

And to make matters worse, Rhona's mother began to be stricter on Rhona for fear of losing her too. Rhona's mother began to drink alcohol. And when she did, she would slap Rhona for making the slightest comment. Rhona's mother would punch Rhona and dare her to hit back.

By the age of 17, Rhona had run away. She stayed gone for 15 months – living on the streets. She had some money saved from the life insurance that her mother had taken out on her dad. She used that money to buy food.

Rhona's mom looked for Rhona from time to time. And when Rhona's money ran out she decided to go back home. However, by the time she and her mother had reunited, the mother's dependence on alcohol had worsened. She was kind to Rhona for a few weeks. But Rhona knew that it was only a matter of time before her mother's fuse was lit and her temper would explode like a twelve pack of dynamite. And Rhona, vowed to never let anyone hit her again – up to and including her own mother. She would defend herself until the death.

And so that began the violent streak in Rhona. She learned to hide it well. She went back to school and stayed out of trouble – most of the time. But one day a bully from school decided that Rhona was her next victim. How wrong she was to choose to bully Rhona!

Sara Parker was her name. She walked up to Rhona right after first period. She said, "I like your jacket."

Rhona said, "Thanks."

Sara moved in closer to Rhona – face to face and with an intimidating whisper she said, "No, I mean I like your jacket. I want it and I'm going to get it. Don't be found walking alone after school. If you do, the jacket is mine."

Rhona slightly intimidated said, "We'll see about that!"

Sara said, "Watch and see don't I get your jacket. Watch and cry as I take your jacket from you and wear it everyday right before your eyes."

By this time Rhona was upset. She did not respond to this threat. Instead she just walked away. She proceeded to her second period class. And then she went to the rest of her classes throughout the day. She avoided the lunch area. She didn't want a confrontation with this girl in the school cafeteria.

And while Rhona went to all of her classes that day, she had a hard time concentrating. She had just told herself that she was NOT going to let anyone else hit her – up to and including her mother. Rhona asked herself, 'Does this mean Sara Parker too?' Undoubtedly, the answer was, 'Yes.'

So, Rhona braced herself. She did not try to walk with an entourage after school. She did not take a different route. Instead, when she was far enough away from the school she waited to confront this bully.

When she saw Sara she asked, "What are you going to do to make me give up my jacket?"

Sara hauled off and socked Rhona in her left jaw. Something in Rhona snapped. After recovering from the punch she rushed Sara. Sara hit the ground and Rhona was standing over her, punching her repeatedly in the face until Sara lied there bloody and unconscious.

Rhona got up, spit in Sara's face and left. From that day forward Sara and the rest of the school gave Rhona the "utmost respect." When Rhona walked through the hallways the other students stepped aside to give her room to pass. They let Rhona be the first in the lunch line and Rhona was the first to be chosen on teams for P.E. class (even though she was not that great at sports.).

And although Rhona never had another fight for the rest of her high school career, she had to admit to herself that there was a bit of an adrenaline rush when she fought Sara. She had to recognize the fact that she liked the respect that she'd gotten from something as simple as losing her temper.

After high school Rhona thought that she no longer had to fight – that there was no more anger inside her – that was until she got married.

On February 8, 1979 she met a man whom she thought was the greatest guy in the world. He was tall, dark and handsome. He had a good income and best of all he was kind to her. He treated her like a queen. He wined and dined her, doted her with roses and candy. He constantly paid her compliments. He often told her how much he loved her. And needless to say, Rhona was mesmerized by his charm. She fell head over heels in love with him and six months later she found herself hearing those infamous words of the minister, "Do you take this man to be your lawfully wedded husband? To have and to hold? To honor and obey? To love and to cherish, from this time forth till death do you part?"

She said, "I do."

So did he. And so they were married.

For the first six weeks of their marriage, her new husband Carl Tillman continued to do the things that won Rhona's heart. He even went as far as to fix her breakfast in bed.

But then around the seventh week Carl came home with bad news. "Rhona, I lost my job."

Rhona was shocked. She couldn't believe that a man who was so dedicated, a man who was so professional, a man who was so punctual and well respected could lose his job! Rhona was dumbfounded. Up to this point Rhona had not worked outside the home. And she had to admit that she had become spoiled rotten. Still she searched her spirit to try and figure out how he could have lost his job and what she could do to help. She wanted to be there for him just as he had been there for her.

After getting over the initial shock, Rhona managed to muster up the words, "How did that happen?"

Carl said, "Well, they said that they were downsizing. They got one of those computers to do my job and so they just didn't need me anymore."

"Wow," Rhona said.

'What will we do now?' she wondered.

So, Rhona started working at Blue Star Restaurant down the street from her house. She waited tables. Her husband told her that she might as well work now since he had taken care of her for so long while she didn't work. He told her that it was his turn to stay home. This angered Rhona a little but her temper had not flared up …yet.

After working for six months, Rhona was frustrated. Her husband still had not found a job and the income she made from the restaurant just barely made ends meet. What's worse is that Rhona would come home to a filthy house and her husband sloppy drunk on the couch with the remote control in his hand. Not to mention that he reeked of urine because many times he was too drunk to make it to the restroom.

Today was the last straw. Rhona's marriage took a turn for the worse and from this point forward her seemingly mild mannered demeanor took a downward spiral.

After a stressful night at work, Rhona couldn't wait to get home. She wanted to plop right down on the couch. Once she arrived, Rhona stuck the key into the lock and turned it. The door opened and she walked in. Rhona looked around and saw the beer can on the table. She had asked him time after time not to put the beer can or any cups on the coffee table without using a coaster. She thought to herself, 'Look at this trifling, fat, slob. Too drunk to get up and use the bathroom. Wearing the same t-shirt and blue jean shorts that he's worn all week. He put this on Monday and it is now Friday. He stinks…HE REALLY STINKS. LOOK AT HIM. JUST LOOK AT HIM. ALL OF THIS FILTH. ALL OVER THE ROOM. TRIFLING SLOB.'

    Before she knew it, Rhona yelled at the top of her lungs, "**GET UP! YOU STINK!**"

    Carl didn't respond. He was in a drunken stupor. So Rhona moved in closer. She yelled in his ear, "**GET UP YOU STUPID, TRIFLING, DRUNKEN SLOB! GET UP AND CLEAN UP THIS FILTHY APARTMENT!**"

    Carl opened his eyes and looked up at Rhona. In a somewhat incoherent manner he smiled and said, "Oh, Hi honey. Are you upset about something?"

    By this time Rhona was fuming with anger. She was breathing heavily, her face and her eyes turned fireball red. She looked around the room to find the closest thing to her. It was a vase that someone had given them as a wedding gift. She picked it up and broke it over his head. Carl jumped up off of the couch. He staggered. Then she rushed at him the same way she had done Sara Parker back in high school. He fell to the floor. Rhona began punching him in his face. She scratched him and bit both his ears and lips until they bled. As he screamed in agony she realized what she was doing and stopped.

    Carl had a swollen bloodshot black eye, swollen ears and lips. It's a shame because he was too drunk to even defend himself. He didn't even push her off of him.

And Carl, needless to say was shocked by all of this. He thought to himself, 'This is not the woman I married.' She was so sweet and loving and kind and respectful. She didn't seem as if she had a violent bone in her body. Now look at me: all beaten and bruised. Yet, I love her too much to hit her back. And, to be honest I am a little frightened by her rage. What am I going to do now?"

These violent attacks went on for the next 15 years. Different things would set Rhona off. It was sometimes the least little pet peeve. Like the time her husband made a smacking noise while eating. He was just about to compliment her on how delicious the meal was when she hauled off and slapped him across the face. "How many times have I told you to close your mouth when you chew? You're so rude and you sound disgusting," Rhona angrily spurted.

Carl and Rhona never had any children. Carl said that he wanted to work things out between them before they had children. The fact of the matter was that Carl couldn't bear to bring children into such a violent dysfunctional relationship.

So, after fifteen years of Rhona's explosive temper Carl couldn't take it anymore. Living with Rhona was simply unbearable. So, without notice Carl moved out and filed for divorce. And five years later Rhona and Carl's divorce was final.

And so there she was. Twenty years older – single, divorced, lonely...and still angry. Sure she went back to school so that she could support herself. In fact she obtained an associate's degree in accounting, a bachelor's degree in Social Work, a master's in business and she's working on her doctorate in Political Science.

Yet with all of her education, she was still unable to overcome the one thing that consumed her. She could not conquer the demon that forced her to lose control. She was filled with rage. She couldn't help it. The fact of the matter is that when she would smile and say, "Don't make me angry. You wouldn't like me when I'm angry," she really wanted help. Every time she said that, she was reaching out for help. She didn't know what else to do.

Everyone at work had heard about Rhona and her anger. And most of her coworkers were intimidated by her temper. They wouldn't dare come to her directly to suggest that she needed help. So, one of the Christian colleagues anonymously placed a flyer on her desk. It was about a support group for women who have problems managing their anger. She read it and thought, 'Oh there's a meeting tonight.'

And so she went. When she got there the group had just formed a circle to pray. Rhona thought to herself, 'Oh, I didn't know that this was a Christian group. Well, I'm not a Christian so I better just leave.'

Rhona headed for the door. But the group facilitator saw Rhona turn around to leave. She yelled out, "No, don't leave. We have a place for you right here next to me!"

Rhona nervously smiled and slowly paced toward the circle and stood next to the leader. The group leader and Rhona clasped hands, "Okay, now everyone join hands." And they prayed.

This was the beginning of Rhona's turn around. She learned a lot from the group. She first learned about what the Bible says in relation to anger. The head of the group proceeded with the lesson. "Let's turn to Proverbs 25:24.

Okay what does it say? Let's read it together. It says, "It is better to dwell in the corner of the housetop, than with a brawling woman and in a wide house."

"Okay now let's go on to Proverbs 22:24-25. It says; well lets read it together: "Make no friendship with an angry man; and with a furious man thou shalt not go; Lest thou learn his ways and get a snare to thy soul."

"We went over this one last week. Who can summarize this for those who weren't here?"

One of the women in the group raised her hand. She explained that verse 24 means that it is difficult to live peaceably with someone who is constantly angry and striking out. She said that verse 25 says that if non-violent people continue in the company of violent people they too will take on violent characteristics.

All this time Rhona knew she had a problem. She knew that many of the problems in her marriage stemmed from her own anger. However, she still never really understood why her husband left her. She felt like he should have tried to work it out.

But then she thought of Carl's many attempts to work things out through talking. He even suggested counseling. He even admitted his drinking problem. But Rhona was never moved by his efforts. Instead, she immediately saw Carl as the enemy trying to patronize her. So she let her fists do the talking for her.

Now, she finally realized what made her husband feel as if he just couldn't take anymore. It occurred to her how much he really loved her. He loved her enough to never defend himself. He loved her enough to leave so that he would not hit her. He knew what it felt like to be the victim of physical pain. He didn't want to put her through that. This stunning revelation was most unbearable for Rhona. She broke down into tears.

And she continued to attend the group sessions. She was there faithfully, every week – on time. And during that time she learned about what Ephesians 4:26 says, "BE YE ANGRY, AND SIN NOT: let not the sun go down upon your wrath: Neither give place to the devil."

Rhona thought to herself, 'Wow! I have gotten angry, sinned, let the sun go down on my anger and given place to the devil lots of times.'

At that point Rhona repented of her sins to Christ. She accepted Him as her personal savior. Through Christ she learned that sometimes repenting to the person we've wronged brings healing for the parties involved. So, she called her ex-husband.

She asked him for forgiveness. He forgave her and told Rhona that he had gotten saved two years after he had left Rhona. He stopped drinking and started his own construction business. He said that the money was really good. He also told Rhona that he still loved her and he missed almost everything about her – all except for the violence. She understood and apologized again. She said that she still loved him too.

So, they decided from that point forward to take things slowly. Rhona decided to continue to attend the anger management classes. She also agreed to attend a weekly Bible study at the church where Carl attends. They said that they'd see what happens from there…

MEMOIR NUMBER FOUR

Name: Omar Levi

Occupation: Ordained Minister of the Gospel - pastor

Age: 57

Sin: Whoremongering and idolatry

Struggle: hypocrisy and heresy

    Omar Levi, Reverend and Pastor as he is most often called, just finished a 12-week crusade. He traveled from Missouri to Virginia, to California to Alabama and then to Chicago. He was so tired. After "ministering" the Word of God he felt drained. But then again, anyone would feel drained after four hours standing before the people of God to 'preach the Word' – so-to-speak and then returning to his room for a cocktail with one of the loose women in the congregation. It's strange how he never takes his wife along with him on these "crusades." Maybe that's because he doesn't want her to know about his escapades in these other cities.
    And she doesn't seem to be concerned about staying behind as he travels the globe. She has her own "extracurricular activities" at home. She takes care of church finances, the church school and she works out. No, I mean she really works out. She has a "friend on the side" as well.

    You should see their church. It's nothing extravagant. The ceiling, floors and walls are puckered from water rotting. The restrooms are filthy. And you can smell mold growing in one of the classrooms.

They never cease to collect an offering. At least three times during each service they request money for this and money for that. They send the members on a guilt trip if they don't have money for the offering. They even speak against the prosperity of those who fail to surrender an offering, "If they have money and don't give Lord God, let their finances be hindered for their disobedience."

And all while they say these things they live in a grandeur mansion. It is a five bedroom, three baths, living room, dining room, kitchen, second floor, basement and a three-car garage. The house is filled with the most expensive furniture. They only drive the best cars – Infinity, Lexus, Mercedes, Hummers. You name it – they drive it.

All of this wouldn't be so bad if the ministry were growing. But it's not. Instead, the people suffer financially while the "leaders" and those who are closest to them prosper to the utmost.

Only those with money or other gifts, talents or knowledge are around the pastor and his wife. They don't have much to do with those who are poor. They don't help them much. It's the, "What-can-you-do-for-**ME**?" syndrome.

And don't you dare tell them that they are in error. Then you are labeled as someone who is coming up against authority. You are called rebellious, insubordinate, into witchcraft or told that you have an "evil spirit."

It is difficult to determine how these two will be delivered from their reprobate minds. Yet, what will those do who fall victim to their "manipulative forces?"

First of all, Pastor Levi and his wife should both repent. And, they should repent not just to the God that they say that they serve and love so much. They should also repent to the wounded souls that they have hurt and stagnated. They should repent before the entire congregation.

Then, they should take actual steps toward moving forward. They should not continue in the sins that they practice. Cutting sinful ties is a good start. Renewing their vows to one another and starting over would help if they don't plan to get a divorce. At the same time they both have Biblical reasons to get a divorce (as if they really care about what the Bible says). They also have three children. They should deeply talk to them and find out how their antics have effected their children's lives.

For the Word of God says in the book of Matthew chapter 23 and verses 13-15, "But woe unto you, scribes and Pharisees, hypocrites! for ye shut up the kingdom of heaven against men: for ye neither go in *yourselves*, neither suffer ye them that are entering to go in. Woe unto you, scribes and Pharisees, hypocrites! For ye devour widows' houses, and for a pretense make long prayer: for therefore ye shall receive the greater damnation. Woe unto you, scribes and Pharisees, hypocrites! For ye compass sea and land to make one proselyte, and when ye is made, ye make him twofold more the child of hell than yourselves."

According to the King James Version of the Bible the meaning of these scriptures is simple. "Ye shut up the kingdom of heaven against men," is another way to say that Omar Levi and his wife are a stumbling block for sinners trying to find their way to Christ. Sinners and new saints are seeking salvation through repentance and conversion but Pastor Levi's lifestyle is a hindrance and a bad example.

"Devour widows' houses" means that the pastor extorts, manipulates, and preys on the weaknesses of those who believe in him. He in turn brainwashes them and brings them into debt and bondage by making comments such as, "Give out of your need. If all you have is money for your mortgage give it anyway even if you don't have enough to pay your mortgage. Yes, give it anyway and God will bless you."

Where is that found in the Word of God? But Pastor Levi doesn't care. He manipulates them by misinterpreting the scriptures – taking God's Holy Word out of context thus prostituting the Word of God – making it the GREAT WHORE. Pastor Omar Levi has an outward show of religion and he is at church having a form of godliness but denying the power thereof.

"The greater damnation," is a more severe punishment because the blood of the people is on his hands. Pastor Levi, does that matter to you?

A proselyte is a new convert to a religion, belief or party. Thus where the scripture mentions a proselyte it is referring to how the Pharisees recruited others for their own benefit all in the name of religion. That's what this pastor does. He seeks proselytes for his own gain under the guise of religion.

To the people of God: FEAR NOT! You are released from that bondage. You are loosed from the clenches of Pastor Levi and those like him. The apostle Paul said, "Be ye followers of me, even as I also am of Christ," (I Corinthians 11:1).

So, **FOLLOW NOT ANY LEADER UNCONDITIONALLY**, but rather as stated in I Timothy 6:11,

"But thou, O man of God, flee these things; and follow after righteousness, godliness, faith, love, patience, meekness."

MEMOIR NUMBER FIVE

Name: Sandy Moore

Occupation: Welfare recipient

Age: 22

Sin: Fornication

Struggle: Wanting love but getting in the wrong places and in the wrong way

    When Sandy Moore was born everyone commented about what a beautiful baby she was. She had a tan, caramel-colored complexion. She had big bright hazel eyes, dark curly hair and a smile that would light up a room.

    As she grew older she proved to be an intelligent child. She could walk and was off of the bottle by the time she was six months old. At eight months she could say a few words. She could recognize numbers and the letters of the alphabet by the time she was one year old.

    By the time Sandy entered kindergarten she could write her own name, read three- and four-letter words, and do simple addition and subtraction problems. She was so much more advanced than the other students that the administrators decided that she could skip kindergarten and go right into first grade. And so she did.

    And her intelligence lasted throughout her elementary, middle and high school years. She graduated high school with honors. She was at the top of her class. She also held down a part-time job as a telemarketer. She was a cheerleader, on the debate team and in the drama club. She was a candy striper and she frequently volunteered at the homeless shelter. She attended Sunday School and church regularly.

Upon graduation she had full scholarships from the top schools in the country – including Princeton, Yale and Harvard. Yes. Sandy had a promising future ahead of her. That's why no one could understand how she turned out the way she has – a mother of four children with one on the way and no husband!

I guess it all started when Sandy started college. She chose to attend Harvard. She was only 16 while other students who begin college are either 18 or 19. She was very intelligent. But looking back, Sandy herself had to wonder if she had the maturity to go away to school so far away from home at such a young age.

While living at home her parents were strict. She was not allowed to date or even have phone calls from members of the opposite sex. She was not even allowed to go out on group dates. Sandy's parents were too afraid that she would end up with the wrong boy and he'd get her off focus. And Sandy was an obedient child. So she obliged her parents' wishes. Thus, she used school and extracurricular activities as an outlet.

At the same time she often struggled in her spirit. Sandy felt that her parents just didn't understand her. She felt like having to be the best all of the time was a lot of pressure. She felt that all of the studying and working and volunteering were stressful. She needed a break. She wanted something to do that *she* enjoyed – not just something that pleased her parents.

Everyone thought that she was so sweet and innocent and that she didn't like boys yet. They thought that the boys were just pursuing *her*. Everyone said, "Oh, Sandy's not like that. Sandy is so smart. Sandy is a good girl."

Many parents told their children, "You should be more like Sandy."

But what they didn't know is that although Sandy is really smart – an academic genius – she *did* like boys. She liked them a lot. And just as many other 16-year-olds, she had her eye on one particular boy. His name was Willis Johnson.

Willis Johnson was a track star and a star football player. Sandy's parents didn't know that she and Willis were dating. And well, they were doing more than just dating. Sandy and Willis had started having sex when she was 14 years old. You may wonder how Sandy managed to date without her parents' permission or knowledge. Well, it's simple.

Sandy frequently asked Willis to meet her after her shift ended. This time she had just finished candy striping at the local hospital. She lied to her parents about what time she would get off. And that gave her extra time to spend with Willis.

He came to the hospital. She waited for him outside. Then when they met up they snuck back into the hospital. By Sandy's volunteering she knew which rooms were vacant. Today it was room 514. They quietly cracked the door to make sure no one was there. After finding that the room was empty, they went in and closed the door.

Willis and Sandy wasted no time. They began laughing, giggling, kissing and hugging. Things got hot and heavy and quickly escalated. Before they knew it their clothes were off. And so they did the deed.

After it was over Sandy reasoned with herself. She said that she loved him. She was sure that he loved her – at least that's what he told her. And that was her justification for doing what she did…LOVE.

Their relationship went on until midway into her senior year. At that point she found out she was pregnant. She wasn't worried though. She knew that Willis would be there for her because he loved her as he had said so many times before. She knew he'd marry her. It would be hard but they'd still go to college and accomplish all of their dreams. It would work…right?

Wrong. Sandy had been feeling nauseous. After realizing that she was three weeks late, she took a pregnancy test from the hospital and had tested herself the night before. It came out positive. Sandy was scared but she knew that Willis would comfort her.

So, the next day Sandy went to Willis during 4th period. They had their own private hangout. He began the normal kissing and groping. But today Sandy felt queasy. She pushed Willis away. This was not her normal response to his advances so he asked with shock and a little bit of agitation, "What's wrong?"

She said, "Willis, I'm pregnant."

Willis sat straight up. He said, "Well what are you going to do?"

She asked him, "What do you mean what am *I* going to do? Don't you love me? Aren't we in this together?"

Willis Johnson said with nervousness in voice, "Yes I love you but I never said anything about a baby. You have got to get rid of it. I am going to college next year. And I am not about to put my parents to shame by having a baby right now! GET RID OF IT!"

After that he got up and ran away. Sandy was torn. Her religious convictions held that abortion is wrong. Yet she knew that fornication was wrong also and she did it anyway. Plus, she knew that Willis had a good point. She didn't want to shame her parents either. She wanted to go to college as well. What was she to do?

I'll tell you what she did. She got an abortion. And other than the physical pain it didn't hurt as much as she thought - at first...

Needless to say, this relationship did not last. After the abortion Willis Johnson "broke up" with Sandy. "Broke up" as in avoiding her, not returning phone calls, standing her up at normal meeting places and times.

In some ways Sandy was naïve but she knew how to take a hint. And, Willis was sending her a big one. He wanted her to GET LOST! He even went as far as to date someone else and flaunt her in Sandy's face. He told the new girl that Sandy was promiscuous and tried to tie him down and ruin his life.

Sandy was devastated. In spite of all this she finished out her senior year with honors. She had to. No way could she ever let on to her parents that something had happened that had gotten her off focus. Her parents frequently told her, "Sandy, NEVER LOSE FOCUS. NEVER LET THEM SEE YOU SWEAT."

So, after graduation she enjoyed her summer. Her parents let up some. They were proud of her. Not only had she graduated but with honors, but also with a full scholarship to Harvard at age sixteen! So, they had started allowing her to go out on supervised dates – with a chaperone. They began to trust her a little more. So, they allowed her to choose her own chaperone.

She chose her cousin Bessie. Bessie was 27. She was attractive and successful – but unsaved. In a lot of ways, Sandy admired Bessie. But on the other hand, Sandy knew that Bessie would let her get away with a lot.

And Sandy's parents were not aware of Bessie's "other side." She had a wild streak. And, while she was supposed to be looking out for Sandy, Bessie would be having a good time herself.

At first, Sandy thought she had it made – by picking Bessie as her chaperone. She could, "hang out with the big girls." Little did Sandy know, she was in over her head...

After just one night with Bessie, Sandy realized that there were things about her cousin that she didn't know. She didn't know that Bessie was a heavy drinker. She didn't know that Bessie was a promiscuous bisexual. She didn't know that Bessie was a liar and a master manipulator. And she didn't know that from time to time Bessie experimented with drugs – marijuana, cocaine, heroin, crack, ecstasy and meth.

Sandy began to start drawing back from Bessie. Sandy felt that Bessie was involved in too much. Sandy didn't want to be a part of all this anymore and she was going to tell Bessie the next time they went out.

And so Saturday night came. Sandy was pacing the floor. She knew that her "dear" cousin would be calling at around 9:00 p.m. So, she waited. It was 8:55. Sandy watched the clock. "8:56. 8:57, 8:58, 8:59, 9:00."

And like clockwork the phone rang. Sandy answered, "Hello?"

The response on the other end was, "Hi cuz. It's Bessie. What cha doin'?"

"Nuthin much," Sandy glumly responded.

She couldn't help it. She wanted to tell Bessie that she was staying home this evening. She wanted to tell Bessie that she was not going out with her any more. But when Bessie asked Sandy what time she'd be ready, she told her, "At the usual time."

So, at 10:30 p.m. Bessie rang the doorbell. Sandy's parents opened the door. Bessie was all smiles. Bessie politely greeted her aunt and uncle. She then proceeded to tell them about the "wholesome" fun that she and their daughter had the last time. Bessie told Sandy's parents that they went to Bible study last time. They asked her what the lesson was about and she told them it was Mark and Matthew 24:36. That's because their dates last time were Mark and Matthew ages 24 and 36.

Unsuspectingly, Sandy's parents were convinced and asked no more questions. Sandy came down wearing a long blue jean jumper (she was wearing another outfit underneath).

When Bessie saw Sandy she smiled and politely asked, "You ready?"

Sandy managed to muster up a smile and said with a mousy voice, "Yes."

Bessie laid it on, thick. "Okay, well let's go…well if it's okay with your parents. We don't want to be late for Bible study."

Sandy's mom and dad said, "Oh sure. Absolutely. You guys have a nice time."

Bessie told them, "Oh, we will."

Bessie had every intention to have a good time. And she was sure that her younger cousin would too. Sandy got into the car. Something stirred her spirit. She was anxious, nervous and just outright uncomfortable.

Bessie got in and slammed the door. Sandy had not yet closed her door. Her feet were still hanging outside the car. She was just sitting there. As Bessie was about to put her key into the ignition Sandy exclaimed, "Bessie wait!"

Bessie was curious but she seemed irritated. Bessie frowned and asked, "What's wrong cuz? Close the door so we can go!"

Sandy just sat there. She felt nervous as her body stiffened. She said, "Bessie I'm sorry but I can't go with you. I don't like what's been going on and I'm in over my head. I want to go back in the house."

Bessie by this time, was very aggravated, "See that's why I didn't want to hang out with you in the first place. You are nothing but a whining baby – always ready to run back to mommy and daddy. What is the problem, Big Baby?"

Sandy was upset and annoyed because she thought that even though her cousin Bessie was not doing the right thing, Bessie should not stand in Sandy's way. Sandy thought that her cousin should try to encourage her to do what was right.

Although Bessie's comments hurt her feelings, Sandy told Bessie, "I'm not going this time Bessie."

"Oh yes you are", Bessie told her.

"No, I'm not and you can't force me to. I'll scream and run back into the house."

"I'd like to see you try that from a moving vehicle."

"If you force me to go; when we get back I'll tell my parents about everything you're into."

"Well, I'll tell them all the things that *you* have been doing when we go out. Then they'll see that their sweet little angel is not as innocent as they thought."

With that Sandy got all the way into the car and closed the door.

Bessie drove off. And later that night, the two ended up sleeping with two other guys that they didn't know. Bessie told Sandy that she was sorry for forcing her to sleep with guys that she didn't know. So, as they prepared to leave she told her to take ecstasy. It will impair her sexual appetite. She won't want to sleep with anyone she'll just want to touch a lot and kiss.

Sandy refused…at first. Then "XTC" as it's called, became her drug of choice. Her cousin told her that it was non-addictive. What her cousin didn't say was that it leads to depression and the use of other drugs.

So after, Sandy became addicted to drugs Bessie didn't want anything else to do with her. "What do I look like hanging out with someone who's strung out on drugs?"

Sandy got stoned a lot. Sandy got so stoned that she'd be gone for days. No one knew where she was. One time Sandy was missing for as long as six months.

Her parents wanted some answers. The first person they called was Bessie. Bessie told Sandy's parents that their daughter was in a drug rehab and that she just doesn't understand how that happened. She gave Sandy's parents the address and they went to visit their daughter.

After six additional months, Sandy was released from rehab. At this time she was about 17 years old. Her parents were hopeful. In their minds, there was still time for her to pursue her Harvard degree. They'll just tell the school that there were some personal problems in their family and everything would be fine. But they didn't know that when they would go to pick up Sandy, she'd have some other breaking news for them.

Yes, Sandy was pregnant. Sandy had beat the drug habit but she still wrestled with the lust demon. And, she had slept with one of the guys in the facility. But the news did not stop here. You see, one of the things that Sandy had learned in rehab was to be honest and face up to your responsibilities. And so, Sandy decided to tell her parents about when she first started having sex, her first and second abortions (Yes, the second abortion was after her encounter with Mark age 24.). But, Sandy decided that there would be no more abortions for her. This time she was keeping the baby.

    She couldn't bear the continual nightmares, the haunting thoughts about how she murdered her babies – her innocent babies. She could no longer stand the cries – every time she heard a baby cry she'd think about her own babies and how they must have cried in their spirit as they had their very life sucked out of them. Oh, what agony! Oh, the pain!

    Sandy did go to school. She didn't go to Harvard though. How could she? She had already had two abortions. She didn't want to go the other extreme and have a child just to abandon him/her all in the name of education. So, she went to the local community college.

    Sandy told herself, 'I can always go to Harvard later. But right now my plan is to get my general requirements done here close to home. Then, I'll transfer. She wanted to give her child time to get older. Maybe once her child was older say about five years old, she could attend a bigger college and pursue a more advanced degree. That way she could attend school while her child was in school.

    It sounded like a workable plan. It could happen with a lot of hard work. But Sandy got sidetracked again. She met Everett Jenkins while at the community college. This time she was sure it was love. They really were in love. There was only one problem. While Everett loved her dearly, he was deathly afraid of commitment. He told Sandy time after time that he never wanted to get married. He always said that, even from the beginning. But Sandy thought their love would change things. It didn't.

They stayed together for five years. And five years and three children later (with one on the way) Sandy had a decision to make. She was in a rut. She didn't finish her associate's degree program because she had to keep dropping out of school to take care of the many babies that she kept having.

Everett however, went on to achieve his master's and was working on his PhD. He made a good salary – about $85-90k a year. But he was still not ready to get married.

Yet, Sandy was in a bind. Her parents helped out a lot with the children. But they were tired and wondered why her boyfriend didn't contribute more.

Sandy gave Everett an ultimatum. She told him that she could not go on like this. She loved her children but didn't know how she could make a living by herself with no skills. She wanted him to marry her and help her more with the children.

Everett broke off the relationship. For two years Sandy heard nothing from Everett other than an occasional phone call. Then one day there was a knock at the door. Low and behold it was him – Everett. He apologized. He said that he missed her and wanted his children. He said that he'd been through some things and he's now ready to commit.

Sandy gave it some thought and decided to marry Everett. And so they were married. But they still had much to work out. Sandy did not know that Everett was controlling and manipulative – less known – physically abusive (maybe that's the real reason that he didn't want to commit).

After five years Sandy had enough. First, she left her husband and then she divorced him. She vowed to never speak to him again...

It had been two years since the divorce. Sandy was progressing well. Her kids had gotten older. She had gone back to school and had attained a computer technology certification. She was making $45,000 per year. Her children were happy and so was she. Except one thing - there was something missing in her life. Sandy didn't know what it was.

But her oldest child had become friends with a child who attended the local church. Her son had started attending church regularly with his newfound friend. He invited his mother to attend with them one Sunday and so she did. And she enjoyed it.

Sandy liked to call the services "refreshing." And after attending regularly as a visitor for about one year, Sandy joined the church. She not only decided to become a member of the church but she accepted Christ as her personal Lord and Savior. She began attending Bible studies, Sunday school, and prayer services. Yes, Sandy was well on her way down the road to salvation.

What Sandy didn't know was that her son (who was also falling in line with God's plan) had started inviting his father, Everett (who was actually his stepfather but the only father the child had ever known) to church as well. Like most kids he wanted to see his parents back together.

After his dad joined the church, Everett decided that he wanted to give it a try again. Sandy agreed. The family went through counseling. It was in counseling where they learned Mark 10:7-9, "For this cause shall a man leave his father and mother, and cleave to his wife; and they twain shall be one flesh: so then they are no more twain, but one flesh. What therefore God hath joined together, let not man put asunder."

Sandy, Everett and their children prayed a lot. They made no immediate changes (like moving in together right away etc.). But, after about one year the family was back together. They were restored, refreshed and refurbished. They were going strong with the love of Christ as their sure foundation.

MEMOIR NUMBER SIX

Name: Katy Lynn Matthews

Occupation: Student

Age: 19

Sin: Backbiting and Gossiping

Struggle: Bridling her tongue

As long as she can remember Katy Lynn Matthews has been a gossiper. Everyone calls her for the latest news about everyone else's business. From the time she was in kindergarten she knew everything from who was still wetting the bed to who was still sucking a pacifier or breastfeeding.

As she got older her mouth got her into trouble a lot. Like the time she was in seventh grade and she ended up getting into a fight (or getting beat up is more accurate) because she spread rumors about Sally Wilson sleeping with a boy. When Katy Lynn was confronted her only response was, *"Well, it's true!"*

And that comment cost her. She suffered a black eye and a swollen lip. She was in bad shape.

After things had gotten so bad, Katy's mom decided to send her to another school. Her mom told her, "I'm taking you out of your old school. But Katy, when you go to Baldrige you must turn over a new leaf. You can't be in everyone's business. You can't talk about everyone. Be nice."

Well, Katy tried to do what her mother asked. For her first month at her new school, Katy stayed out of trouble...until she heard what she called, "breaking news."

She was told that Johnson Pruitt (John, as the kids called him) was going to be kicked out of school. She tried to resist the urge to find out why. But when she'd ended up inside the principal's office one day at the same time as he – she couldn't help overhearing.

And when it was over she walked up to him. She made it her business to let him know how sorry she was that he'd be expelled for exposing himself to three girls inside the girls' bathroom. His face turned beet red and he walked out.

Katy had made a few friends at this new school. And the conversation had come up. They didn't know what had happened. They wanted to know. They seemed so upset. So, Katy decided that she would help them.

And right there at the lunch table during the second half of fourth period, Katy blurted out, "I'll tell you guys what happened."

And thus the vicious cycle began again. It was at that point that Katy decided that she couldn't beat this thing. She told herself, 'Well if you can't be good, be good at it.' And so she did.

She began spreading rumors, befriending people only to reveal their deepest darkest secrets. She was merciless. She must have never read the scripture that tells us that we must reap what we sow. And, by this time Katy had gotten so good at spreading gossip and backbiting that no one could figure out that she was the source.

Until one day she'd met her match. A new student came to Baldrige – Casey Kaitlin. Casey walked into Katy Lynn's English literature class. She had red hair with rosy cheeks. She looked innocent. Katy thought to herself, 'New blood.' Katy was ready to move in for the kill.

Katy's plan was simple. I'll be friendly, get to know her, get her to trust me. Then, I'll figure out what makes her tick. I'll find out the most intimate details about her life and then ...BOOM! I'll drop the bomb on her. She'll never know what hit her.

It was sad. Katy didn't even know why she was like this. What made her want to taint people's reputations? She was out of control.

It wasn't long before her whole plan backfired. Instead of Katy approaching Casey it worked in reverse. Casey came and sat right next to Katy Lynn. This was a little surprising to Katy but she wasn't going to be stopped. Casey was more aggressive than she looked. She said, "Hi. I'm Casey."

Katy attempted to introduce herself. "Hi, I'm –"

Casey immediately interrupted her, "I know who you are. Listen, you seem like a cool person to hang out with. Here take my number down. Call me tonight."

Well, now Katy was a little more intimidated, yet encouraged. She was almost haughty. She thought to herself, 'That was easy. She already knows me and trusts me enough to give me her phone number. I'm on a roll here. Now all I have to do is get her to open up over the phone.'

So, Casey and Katy began to hang out more and more over the next couple of months. But what Katy didn't know about her new friend is that she was a heavy drinker. But by Katy being a good friend she'd never let Casey drink alone.

So, Katy and Casey, one day after school when both their parents had to work late drank half a bottle of scotch. And needless to say, they were more than just a little tipsy. They were toasted, drunk.

They started giggling and began playing "Spin the Bottle and Truth or Dare." Casey dared Katy to tell something really personal about herself. And although Katy was drunk she wasn't stupid. She took the dare. And Casey dared her to kiss her. Katy said, "Oh. That's easy."

She walked right over and kissed Casey on the forehead. Casey smiled to herself. But on the outside her face was expressionless. She looked at Katy with a blank stare. All of a sudden she yelled, "I can't believe that you're a lesbian."

Katy thought Casey was joking. But she said it again, **"YOU ARE A FREAKIN' LESBIAN!"**

"NO I'M NOT! I was just accepting a dare!"

"But you wouldn't have accepted the dare if you weren't at least a little bit *funny.*"

After arguing about this for about fifteen minutes Casey said, "Okay, let's just squash this."

And so they did…for the moment. But the next day it was all over school –"Katy Lynn Matthews is a lesbian."

As she walked down the halls people just stared. Some whispered. There was vulgar writing on the bathroom walls. She was devastated. Because of this incident she and Casey ceased to be friends. But that still didn't cure Katy Lynn of the vices of gossiping and backstabbing.

She did cool down for a while. She waited until she went to college. Then she went full speed ahead.

She was okay until there was a guy in her Chemistry I course that she was really interested in. His name was Terence McCaid. At first he seemed to be really interested in her as well.

They chatted for three weeks during and after class – getting to know each other. And at the beginning of the fourth week he asked for her phone number. She gave it to him. He said he'd call her the same night. It was a Monday.

They talked for about one hour that night. Then they both decided that they had been on the phone long enough. They both had studying to do. So, they decided to talk to each other the next day.

By Wednesday, Terence had asked Katy out to dinner that Friday. She accepted. She was excited and looking forward to their date on Friday.

Katy had to admit that she really liked Terence. He was handsome, charming, considerate and he really listened to her. She was sure that he was the type of guy that she wanted to spend the rest of her life with. What she didn't know was that Terence was not ready to get serious with anybody right now, and Katy found that out the hard way.

There was something else that Katy didn't know. A beautiful, new student had enrolled in Terence's English Composition I course. She had beautiful skin, beautiful hair, a great body and a sweet personality.

And that's why Katy was dumbfounded when Friday rolled around and she got the old, "no call – no show," routine from Terence. She wracked her brain trying to figure out what happened. 'Maybe he's sick. Maybe he was in a car wreck. Maybe he had some family emergency. Maybe I should call him to make sure everything is okay.'

Katy called Terence at home – no answer. She called his cell phone. He didn't pick up. She left a message. She paged him. She called him at work and they said he wasn't there. She called his dorm and he was not there either.

'Hmmmmm,' Katy thought. Where could he be? Oh well, I've left messages. He'll call back. In the meantime, I'm not going to sit around the house waiting for him. I'm going to the mall.'

Katy called a few friends and they headed for the mall. As they drove up, lo and behold guess who they saw leaving the movie theater. It was none other than Mr. Terence McCaid and a mysterious female.

Katy Lynn was furious. Here she is concerned about him, thinking something was wrong and here he is out on a date with someone else – on the very night that *she* was supposed to be out with him. Katy was glad that she never mentioned Terence to her friends. She would have really been embarrassed if they'd recognized him and that he was out with someone else.

But still, Katy Lynn felt that she had to do something to avenge the situation. But what? Then, it hit her. Subconsciously she decided to resort to her old ways. 'I'll tell everyone that she has some horrible STD or that she used to be a man or that she is a cross dresser. I'll do something to make him repulsed by her and make him want to come back to me and then I'll let him come back only to humiliate him and dump him.'

And so she did. Katy Lynn found out this unknown woman's name. It was Marianne. She was from South Dakota. She didn't know anyone here.

This time Katy didn't try to befriend her first. Instead she didn't choose just *one* of the horrible lies. She combined them. She even went as far as to write the horrible information on the wall of the women's restroom, "Marianne Donalee has STDs and she used to be a cross dressing man."

She sneaked into the men's room and wrote the same thing. The next morning Terence was the first to enter the stall where Katy had written the dirt about his new girlfriend. He was shocked, appalled, disgusted.

By the time he got to chemistry class, he wasn't the same. He was looking at the floor when he walked in. He sat in his usual chair – right next to Katy Lynn.

"What's wrong Terence? Is everything okay?"

"Everything is fine. Oh by the way, I couldn't take you to the movies last week because something came up."

Katy mumbled under her breath, "Oh, I'll bet something came up."

"What was that Katy?" Terence inquired.

"I said, what came up?"

"Just – something. Look, I'm not feeling too well. I'm leaving class early today. Will you take notes for me?"

"Sure," said Katy most agreeably.

That night Terence called and apologized to Katy for standing her up on their date. He promised to never do that again. And so he rescheduled their date for the following Friday. Katy told him that she'd go.

Meanwhile, someone in English Comp I had made a rude crack to Marianne about what was written about her. Marianne's face turned red. She got up and ran from the class. She was extremely embarrassed. She ran all the way out of the building and onto the parking lot. She kept going until she got to her car. Then, she opened the car door, plopped down into the driver's seat, slammed the door and just cried. "Who'd do such a thing? And why? I just got here," she sobbed, "I don't even know anyone here. Who'd want to hurt me? I'll find out who did this!"

And Marianne vowed to find out who had written those horrible lies about her on the bathroom walls. She was infuriated.

After Marianne had calmed down, she went to Terence and told him what happened. Well, actually she called and left a message because he refused to be seen with her.

Later Marianne realized something. Marianne had proof of what Katy Lynn had done. And if Katy had investigated Marianne more thoroughly, Katy would have known that Marianne was a dispatcher for school security. That meant that Marianne was in charge of watching the school security cameras and reporting to the campus security guards any suspicious activity.

The day after Katy had written that filth on the bathroom stalls Marianne saw the tape. Marianne saw someone writing and zoomed in to see what he or she was writing. She immediately made a copy and showed it to Terence when he decided to meet with her in an undisclosed location.

Terence apologized to Marianne for treating her so terribly and believing something like that without even talking to her about it first. Then, they decided to beat Katy at her own game. They knew that if Katy had ever done anything like this before, she'd never do it again.

Marianne and Terence both knew the guy who was in charge of the big movie screen in the campus lunchroom. They knew that most students are in the cafeteria between the hours of 12:30 and 1:30. So, they decided that they'd show the videotape at that time. To make it even better, Katy would be there too.

And so, at 1:00 p.m. the next day they showed the tape. Katy Lynn's face turned beet red. She tried to make a mad dash from the cafeteria but there were students blocking every exit. So, she just stood where she was and just cried. She screamed, "That's not me! **That's not me! THAT'S NOT ME!**"

No one believed her. She was horribly embarrassed. And that's not the worst of it. Katy lost Terence as a friend. He was convinced that she was just a horrible person and he refused to speak to her again. He even dropped the chemistry course. He said that he wanted to take it next semester when he knew Katy wouldn't be there.

Katy Lynn spent the rest of her college years trying to live this down. And what made her feel even worse is that her little plan backfired. Not only did Terence and Marianne get back together, they got married two weeks after they graduated college.

To all of the talebearers out there, **THINK BEFORE YOU SPEAK!** When we are not careful with our words, gossip, backbiting or just spreading lies, we are guilty of murder – deep emotional, mental murder. Harsh wreckless words injure the spirit and the innermost parts of the soul. Remember Proverbs 26:22 which says, "The words of a talebearer are as wounds, and they go down into the innermost parts of the belly."

MEMOIR NUMBER SEVEN

Name: John Redman

Occupation: High School Football Coach

Age: 33

Sin: Covetousness

Struggle: Hating to see someone else blessed

"Good morning, Mr. Redman," was the first thing he heard as he proceeded down the halls of Lathan High School. On a daily basis he was politely greeted as he walked down the halls. He quickly threw his hand up in the air in quick response.

'I'm in a hurry. I don't have time to stop and chat,' he thought to himself. He had homeroom for first period and he didn't want to be late.

Most of the teachers at Lathan would label Mr. John Redman as cynical, pessimistic and rude. He always had something negative to say. He was generally condescending, critical, controlling and manipulative. If he didn't get his way he would have a "tantrum" or a "pouting session."

"Most of us just leave him alone when he gets that way," said one of his co-workers.

But John didn't describe himself that way at all. John frequently said, "I just know that I'm right. I can't help it if others don't realize that. And it's frustrating to me when they don't."

That's probably why he had three failed marriages, nine children that he has virtually no relationship with and lives on a salary that is just below poverty level. He has to pay child support for all of his children and neither of his wives would even consider having him back.

His first wife, Lindsey was beautiful and loving. She was the most kind and patient woman that John had ever known. Yet, he supposed that she was loving and kind enough for him to have multiple affairs. She loved him but she decided that after ten years she just couldn't take it anymore. She left him and sent the divorce papers to him in the mail. Because he didn't want the divorce, he didn't sign the papers nor did he show up for court. So, his wife won by default – she got everything she wanted in the settlement.

John was crushed. But he felt that she had been warned. He told her from the beginning that he had a problem controlling himself around other women. He told her, "It's not my fault that you thought you could change me!"

He didn't realize that he was being totally insensitive. Let alone, dishonoring his vows and simply not even trying to do his part to strengthen his marriage. He wanted to have his cake and eat it too. Not to mention that he was insanely jealous about everything that she desired to do (which stems from his own guilty conscience).

He didn't want Lindsey to say hello to other men. He didn't want her to work outside the home because other men will be there and may notice her and try to steal her from him. He didn't want her to go out to eat with her girlfriends because he feared that she'd be scheduling a secret rendezvous with some other man. He didn't want her to go back to school because he felt that she'd try to leave him if she got too high-minded.

Well, needless to say, John reluctantly ended this marriage. But he eventually met someone else and married her. But since he had not worked out the problems from his first marriage he repeated the pattern. And so, the second marriage also ended in divorce on behalf of the wife. Then it happened again a third time.

By this time John was cynical about marriage, women and life in general. Yes, he was blaming others instead of looking to himself as the source of his ship wrecked life.

And to add to his horrible disposition, he was racist. So he hated women, and other ethnic groups. If they were blessed with anything he felt as if they were flaunting it. He felt as if they didn't deserve it. He wondered why they get to have so much when he has very little. He hated them and fumed with discontent.

Most people could see the anger on his face. He seldom smiled. He often scoffed at people when they talked about their blessings.

He lived in a tiny, crowded one-bedroom apartment. He used to be wealthy but after nine children and monthly garnishments for child support he was left with very little for himself. And so he was angry and bitter.

One day at work he noticed that one of his coworkers had gotten a new car. It was a shiny candy-apple red 2005 Ford Mustang. It glistened in the sunlight. The rims (spinners by the way) shimmered.

This colleague happened to be an African-American male. This angered Mr. Redman even more. He saw him – Anthony Robinson was his name – the students called him

Mr. Robinson – as he arrived at work every morning since buying his new car.

John Redman watched as Anthony carefully parked his car – far away from other vehicles – those that were older or not in such good condition. Anthony wanted to avoid scratches and dings on his custom paint job.

Anthony was so happy and excited about his new car because it was his first new car since graduating college. Before the Mustang he drove a canary yellow Pinto. The hubcaps were missing and it made a loud noise when he drove it. He could be heard from blocks away before he even arrived at his destination. So, most of Anthony Robinson's fellow teachers could understand his excitement when he drove up in his new sedan. Most were happy for him... all except Mr. John Redman.

By Friday of the first week that Anthony drove his car to work, John just couldn't take it anymore. He sneakily approached Anthony after school. As Anthony pulled the keys from his pocket to unlock the door John Redman walked up beside Anthony and got in his face, "What's with you flaunting your new little fancy car? So what? You have a new car **WOOP-DE-DOO!"**

Anthony backed away from John. He was shocked at John's display of displeasure. Anthony and John usually got along relatively well. This was all new to Anthony. Nonetheless, Anthony calmly told John, *"Hold on – get out my face man!"*

"Oh, I'll get out of your face man – for now," John sarcastically responded.

Anthony told other co-workers about this surprising encounter with John. They were all astounded and couldn't believe that John would do such a thing. After all, they knew that John was cynical but he was never the type to get into anyone's face. Little did they know that they'd be even more surprised at what John did next.

Another week went by. John stopped speaking to Anthony and the other teachers. Instead he sat back and just watched Anthony. He couldn't stop watching how Anthony took pride in this new car. He watched and thought to himself, 'How can a black Negro afford this kind of vehicle? What does he need with a car like that? Especially since I'm driving a 1984 Ford Escort, that needs a paint job, a new transmission and new breaks.'

John didn't know that Anthony was a Christian. Anthony had prayed for a new car. He had asked God for exactly the kind of car that he wanted. Anthony knew of God's promise in Psalm 84:11b which says, "no good thing will he withhold from them that walk uprightly."

And Anthony walks uprightly. But, John didn't recognize that. John was too busy feeling sorry for himself. John had become consumed by his own bitterness and resentment from his own life. He was hurting inside and he didn't know how to deal with it – except to lash out at others. And that's exactly what John did…

That next Friday John went to the parking lot about 15 minutes before the last bell rang. When he thought no one was looking he went over to Anthony Robinson's brand new candy-apple red 2005 Ford Mustang with spinner rims. With a crowbar in his hand John commenced to scratch a racial slur on the hood of Anthony's car. He then took a hammer and began to bash in those shimmering spinner rims.

John had lost control. He didn't just hit the car a few times and run back inside. John was full of envy. And the rage had built up. Before John knew it the bell had rang. He was surrounded by the entire school – students, teachers, faculty and staff. Everyone stared in awe as he simply lost his mind wrecking Anthony's car.

Anthony Robinson was upstairs grading papers. He had opened the window. He heard all of the crashing and smashing noises. He tried to ignore the ruckus but he couldn't. It was just too distracting. He tried to look out the window to see what was going on. But there were too many people outside. They were blocking the view. He put his pen down on his desk and proceeded down the stairs to see what all the commotion was about.

CRASH! BOOM! BASH! Those were the noises that he heard as he got closer. Once he had reached the bottom of the stairs at the front entrance of the school, he noticed that everyone seemed to be gathered near his car. He knew that because he always parked far away. At this point Anthony began to get a little nervous.

"OOOOOOOH NOOOOOOOOOO! WHAT THE – WHAT HAPPENED TO MY CAR?"

Anthony was almost in tears. He was speechless. But when he saw John Redman with the crowbar on the ground and the hammer in his hand – he knew who the culprit was. His distress quickly turned to anger. Yet, he had to hold back. Anthony thought rationally, 'I cannot resort to physical retaliation against a man holding a hammer and a crowbar.'

And so Anthony did not hit Mr. Redman. However, he did call the police. They arrived within two minutes. Because there were ample witnesses Mr. Redman was arrested on the spot.

"Daaaaaaag. Mr. Redman went postal!" said one of the students.

"Yeah. He's buggin' out. I wonder what drove him to the brink," said another student.

Mr. Anthony Robinson pressed charges. The court date came around and Mr. Redman was sentenced to six months in a minimum-security prison and he was ordered to repair the damages to Mr. Robinson's car. He served three months in jail, three months of community service and repaired Anthony Robinson's car.

Remember that at the time of the incident Anthony was a Christian. Mr. Redman was not. So, during the prison term Mr. Robinson used this as an opportunity to witness to Mr. Redman.

The first time Anthony went to visit Mr. Redman, John was not happy to see him. "Prisoner Redman you have a visitor," yelled the CO into the cell.

Redman wondered who it could be. First he thought that it was one of his ex-wives who had heard about the incident. It was all over the news. He thought to himself, 'How could they *not* know? Maybe they've come to reunite with me. Maybe they feel sorry for me and want to get back together. Maybe I still have a chance with one or all of them.'

But when Redman came out of his cell, walked to the room and sat down at the phone booth he looked through the window. It wasn't whom he'd thought. He was disappointed. "Oh. It's you. Warden!"

"NO! Wait Redman! Now the least you could do is sit down and talk to me. After all you are the one who wrecked *my* car for no reason. Not the other way around."

"Well, I guess you're right. Besides, I haven't had any other visitors anyway."

"Now, that's the spirit," Anthony said sarcastically. "The first thing I want to know is why. Why did you do it? Why did you wreck my car? Why the racial slur? I thought we were at least able to respect each other. I thought that there were no problems between us. Did I do something? If so I'm so---."

"No," John interrupted. "It's nothing you did. Well, I mean that you didn't do anything wrong. It's funny. Since I've been in this place I've had lots of time to think. Lots of time. And I realized that I was so full of anger and bitterness because of some of the things that have gone wrong in my own life."

"But why me? Why my first brand new car?"

By the look on Anthony's face and the urgency in his voice, John could see that he had hurt Anthony deeply. Not just by wrecking his car. That's a material, tangible item that can be repaired or replaced (and it was). But through talking to Anthony, John realized something. It was strange. Anthony had a degree of respect for John. He looked at him as a mentor in some ways. But when John wrecked Anthony's car it was as if John had let Anthony down. It was if John had betrayed Anthony. That's what hurt Anthony the most. At the time John didn't see this but not only did John's actions hurt, disappoint and betray Anthony, John had hurt, disappointed and betrayed himself. Even more, John was embarrassed and ashamed. He knew that he owed Anthony an apology.

"Look Ant, I want cha to know that I didn't realize what I was doing then. I wasn't the same man that I am now. When I first saw you here and I told the warden to come, it wasn't because I hate you or just didn't want to see you or not even because you had done something to me. You know that you didn't hurt me. But the real reason that I wanted the warden to take me back to my cell is because I didn't want to face you. I didn't want to have to confront the fact that I was wrong for what I did. I didn't want to have to swallow my pride and say that I'm sorry. But you know what? I was wrong. And you know what else? I am sorry."

John began to weep. Anthony felt a deep sense of compassion for this man who showed such a sincere genuinely repentant heart. And Anthony Robinson and John Redman didn't realize it but this was the beginning of a new friendship. They would become the best of friends. Why? Because John repented (apologized) to Anthony and Anthony forgave John.

Anthony knew that the Bible says in Matthew 6:14-15, "For if ye forgive men their trespasses, your heavenly Father will also forgive you: But if ye forgive not men their trespasses, neither will your Father forgive your trespasses."

From that day forward Anthony visited John in jail until his release. He witnessed to him about the love of Christ. He encouraged John to seek a personal relationship with the Lord. Anthony told John that God knew about all of his troubles, his iniquities (sins), and how hard it was to carry the weight of it all. Anthony told John that he could lean on Jesus because Christ is a burden bearer. Anthony told John about Matthew 11:30 which states, "My yoke is easy, and my burden is light."

And so they were friends well in to their elderly years. They lived to see many great things happen in each other's lives. John saw Anthony get married and was his best man at his wedding. John saw the birth of Anthony's children and was their Godfather.

Anthony saw pivotal moments in John's life as well. John's financial situation improved. John sought the sincere milk of the Word of God and grew with every passing day. He graduated to the meat of the Word – deeper spiritual things. And so he prospered even as his soul prospered.

He prospered so much until God opened the door for him to pastor his own church of a congregation of 20,000 members. John started a crisis center for anger management and he continued his education and was hired on as principal of the local school district where he served for 20 years. He also worked things out with his second wife. They remarried and it lasted for 22 years. John was also able to maintain a cordial relationship with his two ex-wives. Saints, see how God blessed?

Conclusion

With man things are impossible, but with God all things are possible. God wants only the best for us, but we have to obey His Word, His statutes, His commands.

The Word of God says in 2 Corinthians 13:5, "Examine yourselves, whether ye be in the faith; prove your own selves. Know ye not your own selves, how that Jesus Christ is in you, except ye be reprobates?"

Everyone needs to examine his life. Our daily prayer to our Lord should be: "God if there is anything in me that is not like you please take it out right now, in the name of Jesus."

Sadly however, many people sin repeatedly without regard for the God in heaven that is looking down upon them. Many people take salvation and Christ lightly. Some are even bold enough to think, 'Oh I'll sin now, and repent later.' As a result when we sin repeatedly without regard for the Father, he turns us over to a reprobate mind. That means that lets us do whatever we think we want to do. We in turn, become full of sin and we don't care who we hurt (ourselves included). Even more tragic is that with a reprobate mind, we don't even have the desire to seek God anymore. It's almost the point of no return.

It's a shame that many churches teach that it's okay to be saved and keep on sinning. Where does that ideology come from? Where are our morals and values? Where is our reverence and love for the Almighty Creator?

They base this philosophy on the scripture in I John 1:10 that says, "If we say that we have not sinned, we make him a liar, and his word is not in us."

It is my belief that this scripture is referring to sinners. Some people who have not committed certain sins tend to think that they are "OKAY." They don't understand what's so bad about them that they need to be saved. They tend to think that salvation is for those who were really "out there" so-to-speak.

However, Isaiah 64:6 says "But we are all as an unclean thing, and all our righteousnesses are as filthy rags; and we all do fade as a leaf; and our iniquities, like the wind, have taken us away."

So, for those who have not committed as many sins as another person or those who have not sinned on the same magnitude as someone else, bear in mind that your "righteousness" still won't measure up to that of Jesus Christ. No way could you die on a cross for the sake of others. No way could you take the torture without defending yourself. No way could you endure without giving up and saying, "It's not worth it. Let all those horrible sinners die and go to hell and burn for eternity," (which is exactly what would have happened had He not sacrificed His life for us).

Many of us don't realize the impact of sin and how we begin to wither away because of it in our lives. So, it's not okay to sin as a body of believers and keep on sinning and then think that we are justified. WE ARE NOT!

Hebrews 10:26 says, "For if we sin willfully after that we have received the knowledge of the truth, there remaineth no more sacrifice for sins."

Saints of God, we need not think that we can willfully sin, repent; sin, then repent; sin; repent and sin, repent again. Sin is a deliberate act. We know what we are about to do before we do it. And when it comes to sin, we don't have to do it. I Corinthians 10:13 says, "There hath no temptation taken you but such as is common to man: but God is faithful, who will not suffer you to be tempted above that ye are able; but will with the temptation also make a way to escape, that ye may be able to bear it."

Now don't get me wrong, I understand that sometimes we make mistakes and in our own ignorance the enemy uses that as an opportunity to trick us and draw us into an abyss of sin. I'm not talking about that. I'm not talking about when we are victims of rape, violence or molestation. I'm not talking about when someone puts a drug into a drink and then a person becomes addicted to that drug. I don't mean that no one can be forced into prostitution. I am not referring to any of that.

I'm referring to a willful act of sin: adultery for instance, can be prevented. All sins if we head them off at the path can be prevented and we won't have to reap the consequences. Just think about it. Romans chapter six has many references to "sin prevention."

Romans 6:1-2 states, "What shall we say then? Shall we continue to sin, that grace may abound? God forbid. How shall we, that are dead to sin, live any longer therein?"

Saints, let us be dead to sin. Once we accept Christ as our personal Savior, let us realize that he paid the price for us to be "dead to sin." In Him we find the way to stay away from sin.

"Therefore we are buried with him by baptism into death: that like as Christ was raised up from the dead by the glory of the Father, even so we also should walk in newness of life," (Romans 6:4)

We are to have a new life in Christ – "sin-free."

The Word of God tells us, "Knowing this, that our old man is crucified with him, that the body of sin might be destroyed, that henceforth we should not serve sin" (verse 6).

"For he that is dead is feed from sin," as verse 7 explains.

Verse 11 goes on to say, "Likewise reckon ye also yourselves to be dead indeed unto sin, but alive unto god through Jesus Christ our Lord."

The Lord Jesus wants all of us to really get verse 12, "Let not sin therefore reign in your mortal body, that ye should obey it in the lusts thereof."

Verse 13-14, "Neither yield ye your members as instruments of unrighteousness unto sin: but yield yourselves unto God, as those that are alive from the dead, and your members as instruments of righteousness unto God. For sin shall not have dominion over you: for ye are not under the law, but under grace."

Verse 18 tops it all off. It is the icing on the cake. It says, "Being then made free from sin, ye became the servants of righteousness."

Now isn't that GOOD NEWS? Don't you know that we don't have to sin? So, don't listen to the hypocrisy and the heresy that teaches that as saints we are still supposed to sin. The Word of the Living God tells us otherwise. Don't let the Devil fool you.

WORKS CITED

(Contributing Editors). The King James Study Bible. Nashville: Thomas Nelson Publishers. 1988.

http://win-edge.com/RestorationTextOnly.shtml

http://www.exodus-internantional.org/ministry-mo.shtml

http://hartford.about.com/cs/healthcare/a/aaecstasy.htm

http://www.no-porn.com/breakin.html

Pfeiffer, Charles F.; Vos, Howard F.; Rea, John – editors. Wycliffe Bible Dictionary. Hendrickson Publishers. 1975.

Strong, James. The New Strong's Exhaustive Concordance of the Bible. Nashville: Thomas Nelson Publishers. 1990.

http://www.theantidrug.com/drug_info/drugs_ecstasy.asp

Printed in the United States
31721LVS00001B/85-171